For Libby Rose
~ *J.W.*

For my patient family
~ *N.B.*

Text copyright © 1998 by Judy Waite
Illustrations copyright © 1998 by Norma Burgin

*Library of Congress Cataloging-in-Publication Data*
Waite, Judy.
Mouse, look out! / by Judy Waite
illustrated by Norma Burgin.—1st American ed.
p. cm.
Summary: Inside an old, abandoned house a mouse
searches for a safe place to hide from a cat.
ISBN 0-525-42031-2
[1. Mice—Fiction. 2. Cats—Fiction. 3. Stories in rhyme.]
I. Burgin, Norma, ill. II. Title.
PZ8.3.W1355Mo 1998
[E]—dc21 98-5249 CIP AC

Published in the United States 1998
by Dutton Children's Books,
a member of Penguin Putnam Inc.
375 Hudson Street, New York, New York 10014
Originally published in Great Britain 1998
by Magi Publications, London
Printed in Belgium by Proost NV, Turnhout
First American Edition
2 4 6 8 10 9 7 5 3

# Mouse, Look Out!

Judy Waite

illustrated by
Norma Burgin

Dutton Children's Books
New York

The gate no one opened
was rusted and old.
When the wind blew against it,
the hinges creaked and moaned.

And tucked among the cracks
of the ivy-covered wall,
a little mouse was peeping.

Then silent as the sunset,
a shadow came creeping.

MOUSE, LOOK OUT!
THERE'S A CAT ABOUT.

The door no one knocked on
was battered and scratched.
When the wind came calling,
it pounded, banged, and bashed.

And through the broken wood,
so raggedy and jagged,
a little mouse was crawling.

Then down the tangled path,
a shadow came prowling.

MOUSE,
LOOK OUT!
THERE'S A
CAT ABOUT.

The hallway no one stood in
was dusty, damp, and dark.
When the wind came racing,
cobweb curtains pulled apart.
And across the tattered carpet
of frayed and faded patterns,
a little mouse was scurrying.

Then softly through the door,
a shadow came hurrying.

MOUSE, LOOK OUT!
THERE'S A CAT ABOUT.

The kitchen no one cooked in
was grubby, grim, and gray.
When the wind wailed through,
it swept the leaves and sticks away.

And round the piles of pots
and in the long-forgotten cupboards,
a little mouse was searching.

Then slowly down the hallway,
a shadow came lurking.

MOUSE, LOOK OUT!
THERE'S A CAT ABOUT.

The staircase no one used
stretched upward in the gloom.
When the wind came climbing,
its soft breath lingered in the room.

And up the giant steps,
with scrabbling and scratchings,
a little mouse was struggling.

Then slinking up behind,
a shadow came lunging.

MOUSE, LOOK OUT!
THERE'S A CAT ABOUT.

The bed no one slept in
was jumbled up with junk.
But the wind had left the house,
and the room seemed warm and snug.

And in among the mess,
inside the torn, worn mattress,
a little mouse was sleeping.
Then through the quiet room,
something came leaping. . . .

CAT,
LOOK OUT!
THERE'S A
DOG ABOUT.